THE ADVENTURES OF THE DISH AND THE SPOON

MINI GREY

RED FOX

Someone
put a record
on the new
record player.
It was playing
our tune.
How could we resist?
ho
ho
ho
ho
ho

MOONY TUNES
HEY DIDDLE
DDLE
RCHESTRA

The Dish whirled around
on the moonlit ocean.

I didn't know
where we were going,
and I didn't care.

I knew the Dish
would take us there.

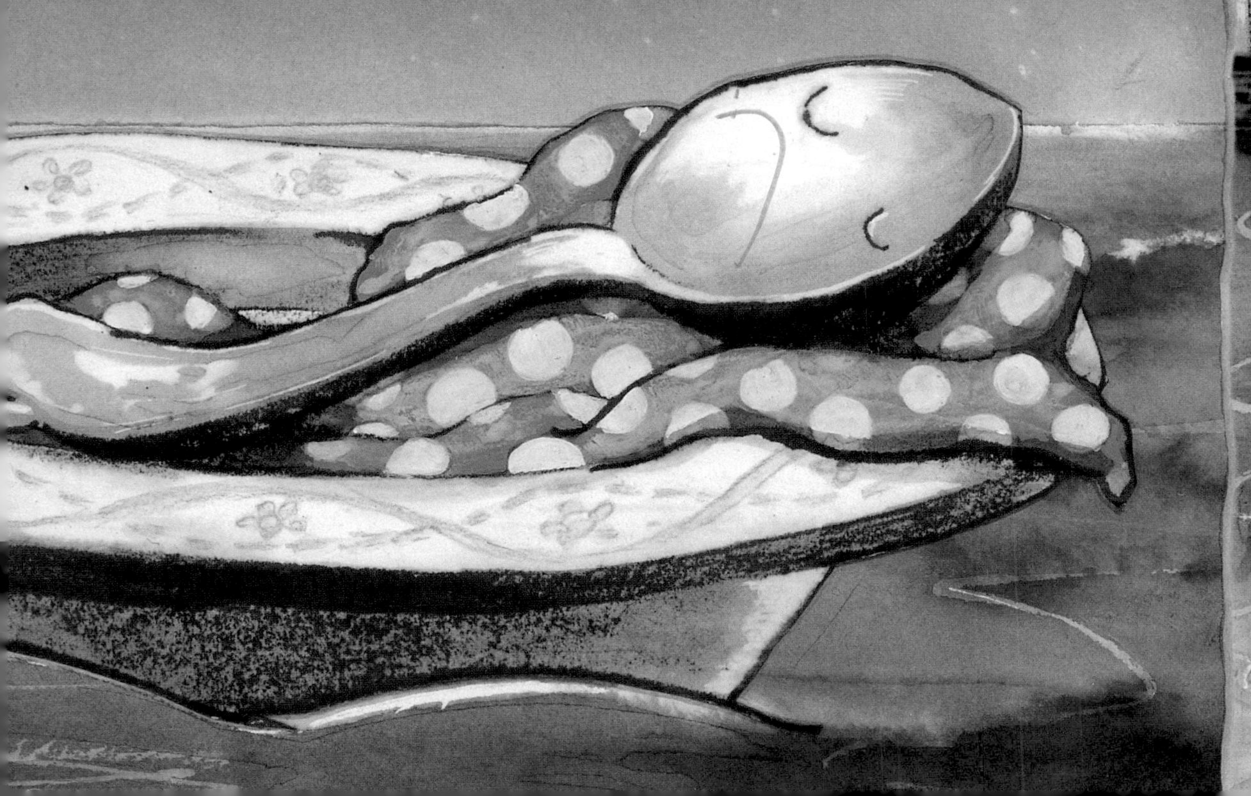

INTRODUC
OUR NEW ACT
the DISH & the SP

We tried our luck
as an act in a
travelling show.

The audience loved us!

We were famous.

The Dish got a taste for the high life.
We bought a motor car.
The Dish shopped for
jewellery and furs.

Soon our money was all gone.

A gang
of sharp
and shady
characters
offered to
lend us some.

They tried to
frighten the Dish.
What could we do?
6.50
We couldn't
pay them back.

"Stop!
Untie the Dish!"
I screamed.
"I've got a plan!"

"No one will recognize us,"
I whispered.
"Just march into the bank
and it'll be over in
no time."

BANK
POLICE

Oh, we were so foolish!
Of course they recognized us.
We'd appeared on posters all
over the country.

We tried using
some of our old tricks
for our getaway . . .

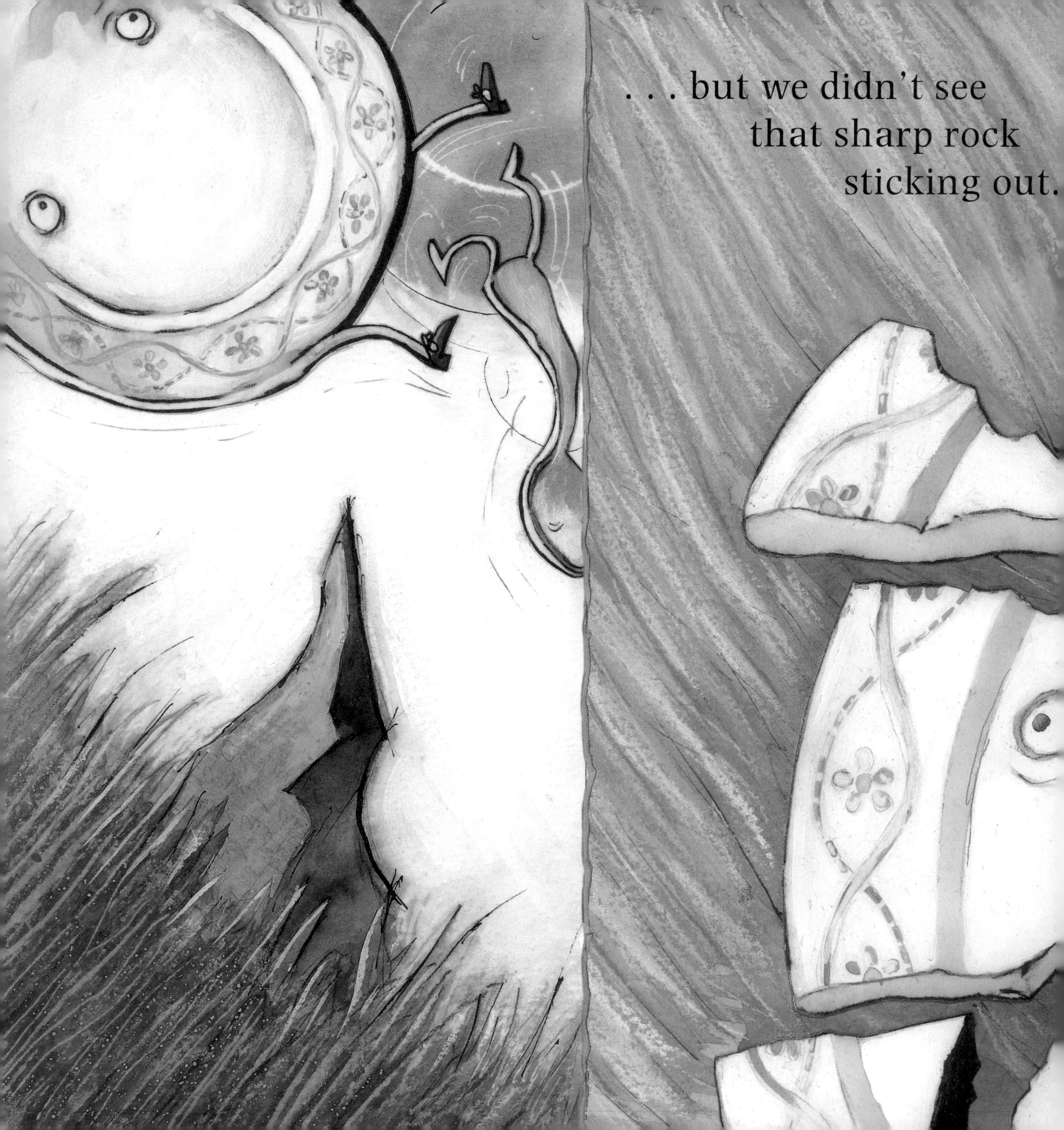

. . . but we didn't see
that sharp rock
sticking out.

"Run while you can, Spoon," breathed the Dish.

But the Dish
was broken
and so was I.

I let them
lock me up
and turned away
from the moon.

DEPORT
Name: the Spoon
Appearance: Oval face
metallic colour
released on bail
HAS DONE HIS TIME
BUGS
YOUR
INSECT

Twenty-five years later,
I'd done my time.

I blinked in the sunny street.
The world had really changed.

What home could there be
for a lonely, broken old
spoon like me?

Then I saw this shop.
"Perfect," I said.

I heard a soft sobbing.
Those faded flowers
looked familiar.

"Dish?" I whispered.
"Is that you?"
"Don't look at me, Spoon,"
she wept. "I am old and cracked,
and my glaze is crazed."

"Dish," I said, "you look just
the same as you did the
June night we ran away."

The Dish sniffed.

Someone had put
a record on the
old record player.

The sound was scratchy,
but we knew that tune.

“Can you remember the old tricks, Dish?”
I asked. The Dish nodded.
“Well, there’s a whole new world out there.
People who have
never seen dishes
do tricks with
spoons.”

THE DISH
AND THE SPOON
Every Night
Admission
FREE

THE ALL-NEW MOONY TUNES ORCHESTRA PRESENTS

Hey Diddle Diddle

featuring

DISH and SPOON as themselves

CAT on Sax

Laughing Dog on DRUMS

COW on keyboard

To the one and only PiPPA

Red Fox • UK | USA | Canada | Ireland | Australia | India | New Zealand | South Africa • Red Fox is part of the Penguin Random House group of companies whose addresses can be found at global.penguinrandomhouse.com. • www.penguin.co.uk • www.puffin.co.uk • www.ladybird.co.uk

Penguin Random House UK

First published in Great Britain by Jonathan Cape 2006
Published in this edition by Red Fox 2007, reissued 2017

013

Printed in China
A CIP catalogue record for this book is available from the British Library
ISBN: 978–0–099–47576–7
All correspondence to:
Red Fox Books, Penguin Random House Children's
80 Strand, London WC2R 0RL

MIX
Paper from responsible sources
FSC www.fsc.org FSC® C018179